CW01086695

CUSTER'S LAST STAND

and other stories

CUSTER'S LAST STAND

and other stories

Harry Wojtczak

ATHENA PRESS
LONDON

Custer's Last Stand
and other stories
Copyright © Harry Wojtczak 2006

All Rights Reserved

No part of this book may be reproduced in any form
by photocopying or by any electronic or mechanical means,
including information storage or retrieval systems,
without permission in writing from both the copyright
owner and the publisher of this book.

ISBN 1 84401 802 4

First Published 2006 by
ATHENA PRESS
Queen's House, 2 Holly Road
Twickenham TW1 4EG
United Kingdom

Printed for Athena Press

For Kieran

With the exception of the immediate members of the author's family, all other characters, and events, in this book are fictional. Any resemblance to actual places, events or persons, living or dead, is purely coincidental

Contents

Custer's Last Stand
A very short Christmas story

D ivorced parents all over the world will be familiar with this scenario. It's Christmas Day. This time it's your turn to host your one and only child for the Big Day.

Of course, this should be dead easy. Shove a turkey in the oven, add some veggies, wait for a few hours and all there is to do is the gravy. Absolutely no problem, even for a marginal cook like this father.

Life is never easy. One-and-only Child informs me that he's had enough roast dinners to last a lifetime and what he really wants is a good old-fashioned fry-up – usual things, bacon, eggs, sausages, toast, etc.

One problem: this is announced on Christmas Eve, and fairly late at that.

Quick summary of the kitchen's contents reveals the worst. Some bacon in the freezer with an unknown expiry date; eggs that definitely have gone past their expiry date; and some malodorous salami which is quickly thrown over the fence for Custer, the dog next door. He has no problems with it what-soever, just gulps it down, wags his tail and waits for the next offering.

Panic is now setting in. Enough time left to buy the goods for this Christmas meal? No worries. Cancel the rest of the appointments for the day.

Screech to a halt outside the local butcher's. Only one lot of sausages left.

'What sort?' I ask.

'Buggered if I know,' is the answer from the customer relations operative, 'but if you want them you'd better be quick. We shut in five minutes.'

That's the sausages taken care of. Now the eggs and the bread.

Both of these seem to vanish at Christmas time, especially on Christmas Eve. Takes a lot of smooth talking to persuade the young lady in the supermarket to rediscover some eggs with an expiry date that would have done credit to the ones I'd just thrown out and a loaf of bread with suspicious blue marks on it. Not to worry, I say to myself, by the time it's toasted nobody will notice a thing. I can always scrape off the sides.

Rushing out of the supermarket, notice some egg rings in the kitchen aids section. These metal objects apparently sit in the bottom of the frying pan, wait for the raw egg to be dropped into the hot butter in which they reside, and within minutes, produce the perfectly formed fried egg. I buy six of these.

Now on the last lap. Back home to peel the potatoes and the onions, grate them, add the egg, pepper and salt and some secret ingredients (anything that's lying around, basically). That'll do for the potato pancakes, or hash browns as the modern generation calls them. All is now ready for the Big Day. As a last thought, get out the corned beef from the fridge where it's been incubating for the last three months and give that to Custer as a Christmas Eve treat.

One thing about Custer: he appreciates home cooking. Corned beef went down a treat. Wags his tail, looks back at me expectantly.

That's it, I think, I'm ready for the morning. A few glasses of wine and…

Wake up at the sound of the front door being opened. Who the hell would be coming round at this time of night? Check the time. Realise it's well into Christmas Day, a point reinforced by the entry of the only son and heir.

A convivial hour follows. Some intimate talk, a few glasses

to lubricate the discussion and then the Christmas Day meal.

Won't say a lot about the sausages and the bacon. They were there as extras. So too, as far as I could gather, were the potato pancakes.

But the toast was as good as you could get anywhere. And the eggs! They were exquisite. Cooked to perfection, perfectly rounded shapes, would have graced the menu of the best restaurants.

But of course this is not a perfect world. By the time my son and heir had finished making verbal love on his phone to his one and only, the eggs were congealing on their plate regardless of my prayers to whatever saint was available and able to keep them in the perfect state that they had been.

However, the aforementioned son and heir finally appears. The perfect fried egg is sandwiched between two pieces of exquisite toast, drenched with tomato sauce, and shovelled into his mouth.

'Like another one?' I ask. 'There are still a few left.'

'Nah,' he says. 'Have to see the girl. Lend me the money for the taxi fare, could you?'

I am now alone with a sinkful of dirty dishes, loads of excess food, thinking, Why, Lord, do I bother? I vow to disinherit my son.

Custer's tail is still wagging. Best Christmas ever, as far as he's concerned. So over the fence goes the bacon, the sausages and the last perfect fried egg. One thing about Custer: he's a real gourmet. Relishes the whole thing. Wish some others would.

Boxing Day. Receive a call from my only son (no longer heir) to thank me for a great Christmas Day. I do not reply.

Still, for me this is another working day. As I leave, I notice a mobile vet turning into the drive of the house next door. I contemplate leaving the country.

Author's Note

This is obviously a work of fiction, as my son would be the first one to confirm. I used poetic licence when I said I did not reply to his call. What father wouldn't?

Incidentally, I did not disinherit him. What's a perfect egg between a father and son?

And for those of you animal liberationalists out there, I can reassure you that Custer has never looked better. The vet was there just to give him his annual vaccination shots.

Only trouble with Custer is that I can't set a foot outside the house these days without seeing that wagging tail and those expectant eyes.

Maybe I should leave the country…

Bo and Arrow

In Ireland he would have been called a gurrier. In Australia, a bit of a larrikin. In most parts of England, probably a bit of a lad.

To the South Bristol Police Force, he was a person of interest, and had been since his arrival in town.

No one was sure where he hailed from. His mother, Marynia, arrived in Bristol in the autumn of 1955. Her sole possessions were one suitcase and her only son. She had believed when they left the refugee camp that there would be a relative or a friend in the big town who would look after them. Sadly, that proved not to be the case. The relative had died, and friends, as so often happens, disappeared at the prospect of a single mother with a child in tow.

But, thanks to the small legacy left by the dead relative, plus help from the local émigré community, she and her son were able to settle down in a small flat (apartment would have been too grand a name) just on the south side of town, in what was known, euphemistically, as a working-class area. And probably would have, had there been enough jobs to go around.

He was in trouble from day one.

At the age of ten, unable to speak a word of English apart from 'yes' and 'no', he was left to find his own way in the sometimes chaotic world of post-war England.

He did it by the only means at his disposal: his fists, and a mind that, if properly fostered, could have generated a credit to his community, but instead became the vehicle for his survival, twisting and turning circumstances to best meet the needs of both him and his mother.

His father had long ago left the scene. No one was sure of who or what he was – some said Polish, some said Ukrainian, most said a gypsy. He left his son just the merest handful of things to remember him by. An ambiguous surname, Kulak. A somewhat swarthy complexion. And the face of an angel. Plus a medal from the Italian campaign in 1944, which a lot of people said had been bought in a jumble sale.

But those were the things people saw on the outside. Within was a gene pool that made him what he really was. First, the rat cunning; survival at all costs; and a fierce loyalty to Marynia, his mother. She was the one who had named him Bohdan (the God-given one). And she was the one to whom he could turn to in times of trouble and give him the love and support he so deeply craved.

Of course, Bohdan proved to be too much of a mouthful of a name for most people, so, soon, it was shortened to Bo.

The second feature of that gene pool was a higher-than-average IQ. Bo could soak up information and knowledge like a sponge. He did that and put it to good use whenever he could. Unfortunately, rarely at school. He detested the place, the uniformity demanded of all who attended, the mindless rules and regulations, the subjects that left him bored senseless, and worst of all, the overbearing and paternalistic attitude of most of the teachers.

In those days, of course, corporal punishment in the education system was a fact of life. And Bo, being the person he was, attracted perhaps more than his fair share. Never one to mask his feelings, his attitude seemed to provoke the worst reaction from his teachers. And, as luck would have it, in that part of Bristol in those days, there were few teachers with the warmth, compassion or ability to foster and develop the latent talent just under the surface of the lad's make-up.

Most of the beatings took place in the classroom. He took them all without flinching; he did not want to give anyone the satisfaction of knowing how much it all hurt. Only Marynia knew; and Marynia and provided the love and support that he so needed.

But as happens sometimes, his reputation within the school community grew; he became something of a cult figure to the other pupils, someone to look up to. The boys all wanted to be his friends and be like him, the girls just wanted him.

And he probably would have made it through school except for one unfortunate incident.

One particular teacher one particular day took exception to Bo's attitude. An ill-directed swipe at the lad's head left the lad with a bruised cheek and a rapidly closing left eye. As usual, Bo did nothing about it. Accepted it as part and parcel of life.

Not so Marynia. When she saw the damage she was beside herself. Normally a shy, self-effacing woman, she decided that this time enough was enough. Despite Bo's protestations she went to the school to confront the teacher responsible. And confront him she did, with words that would have done credit to the best of fishwives.

The teacher made the mistake of pushing her towards the door. At this Bo saw red.

The teacher woke up in a hospital bed with a broken nose, severe lacerations to his face, concussion and a realisation that, perhaps, this time, he had underestimated his target.

Of course, the police were called in to investigate this case of grievous bodily harm. Bo managed to escape the charges when the rest of the class swore that it was an act of self-defence. But the police file on him was now open, and he was a marked man.

He was expelled from school, but to Bo that didn't mean much. Never liked the place anyway.

At that time South Bristol was not a place of high employment. Getting a job with no educational qualifications was not the easiest thing in the world. It was thanks to Marynia, who worked at the local bus depot as a kitchen hand and was well respected there, that he got the opportunity to try out as a bus conductor.

Bo took to the job like a duck to water. Once at work, he was his own boss. Free to express himself as he saw fit, interact with the public, yes, he was in his element. And then, of course, there were the scams. It did not take him long to work those out. A nudge or a wink here or there, a coin pressed into his hand in a certain way, totally ridiculous figures recorded on his ticket machine, and our lad was away.

Of course, this needed the connivance of the bus driver. Soon, all it took was a sudden application of the brake pedal for Bo to know that there was an inspector ahead. But even that was easily solved – a free breakfast or lunch, some cash contribution – everyone was happy.

Except the bus company.

Contrary to popular opinion, these organisations monitor the returns coming in from various routes quite closely. Where Bo was concerned, these seemed to have dropped dramatically. So, inevitably, the police were called in.

This was where Strela appeared on the scene. Daughter of a Russian émigré, her name could be translated as 'arrow'. The diminutive version was Strelka, or 'little arrow'.

She was a regular on one of Bo's runs. Despite a mutual attraction, and a considerable amount of flirting on both sides, Bo was deterred by the wedding ring on her left hand. There are some things even a South Bristol boy does not do. Bo, for all his faults, set great store by his honour.

It was Strelka who alerted him to the fact he had a new regular passenger who seemed to take an extraordinary interest in the number of people on the bus at any one time, their destinations, and the amount of money changing hands. Bo reacted appropriately. The scams were reduced (obviously not completely eliminated – that, as far as Bo was concerned, would be going too far), enough for the investigation to come to a dead end.

But as a result, the friendship with Strelka developed. So much so that in a moment of weakness he invited her back to the flat he shared with his mother – just for a cup of tea, nothing more.

Some women take to each other at first sight, some detest each other immediately. Marynia and Strelka came in the first category. By the end of the evening Bo was left wondering why he had not seemed to say more than a word or two all evening and why he felt like the proverbial invisible man.

The feeling wasn't helped at all by the fact his mother said after Strelka's departure, 'Now that's the sort of girl you should take up with instead of gallivanting around.' Bo pointed out that she was a married lady, to which Marynia replied with a deeply meaningful, 'Hm.'

Life flowed on. Bo got into trouble a few times with the police, mainly on Friday nights after a few beers too many at the local pub and the odd altercation with another patron. But to be fair, Marynia only had to bail him out once, and that was purely because he said he'd been defending some young girl's honour. Exactly from whom was a matter of opinion.

Marynia kept reminding him he should find a girl like Strelka, someone to keep him on the straight and narrow. Bo doubted that was possible.

But Bo and Strelka still saw each other regularly on the bus route, and the friendship deepened.

Bo's passion in life was snooker. If not at work or in the pub, chances were you would find him in the snooker hall. And he was good – maybe not as good as he thought, but still very good. His favourite ploy was to approach any newcomer, put on his most innocent face and ask if a game could be arranged – with a side bet, of course. And, of course, after the initial token loss when the bets would be raised, he cleaned up.

As happens, complaints were raised. At police level. A visit to his flat by the local constabulary produced little, mainly because of Marynia. A welcoming cup of tea, affirmation of her faith in the British justice system, the flat denial that her Bo could have been involved, ' 'cos he was here all the time', and he'd be off the hook.

But Bo would get reproached. Why couldn't he find a girl

like Strelka? Why couldn't he settle down? Give her the grandchildren she yearned for?

Because he was Bo, that's why. And that was the way it would stay.

Jacob Freedman was a big figure in South Bristol in those days. Big in size, big in reputation. Someone to avoid unless you were really looking for trouble.

Jacob really loved his snooker. So it was just a matter of time before South Bristol was to experience what has since been referred to as 'something to remember', a bit of folklore to be passed down though the generations.

The match was to be a best of seven. Stakes were high, very high. Marynia raised some cash to help Bo out, even though she severely disapproved of the whole event. But she made an exception for this one time; she was there in his corner, so to speak.

Things did not start off too well for Bo. His style of play was the same as his nature. Fast and quick. Jacob, on the other hand, took an age over every shot, pondered every move, drove Bo to despair.

In a short space of time, Jacob was 3–0 up with just one frame to win to take out the match. And that seemed like a formality.

A break was called. The match would resume in fifteen minutes. Fifteen minutes to oblivion.

Bo glanced across to where Marynia was sitting. He was surprised to see Strelka next to her, both engaged in what seemed like a very deep conversation.

'Make a good pair, don't they?' came Jacob's voice at his side. 'Your mother and my wife. Still, let's get this over with so we can all get back to our lives, and you can crawl back into whatever hole you came from.'

Sometimes a man needs something to spur him on. That was probably what Bo needed. Played like a man possessed.

Even included a 147 break. He was on fire.

It was Jacob's turn to call time. Needed a moment to get his thoughts together.

That and a few of his thugs to let Bo know the possible consequences of the wrong result.

'Fair enough,' said Bo, and pointed out a few of his own friends in the audience, ones that would back him whatever. No threats, just enough to let Jacob know that the use of force could go either way. It also served as a reminder that the South Bristol Police Force was taking an intense interest in the proceedings – several members were in the crowd that night.

What followed was the stuff of legends. Bo, slightly unsettled by the exchange, began badly. Before too long he was way down against Jacob. Visions of defeat and humiliation stared him in the face.

He fought back as best he could, but in the end, it was left to Jacob to sink the last of the coloured balls and the game and match were over.

Bo called for a short break. Allowable in those days. Especially with the police watching.

Marynia came to talk to him. Typical maternal stuff, told him to do his best. And gave him the sort of advice only a mother can give. He felt better. He looked across at Strelka. She smiled and nodded.

The game restarted.

Jacob sank the first two colours without any problems. Third was trickier, but still put away.

'Hear you've been having a few problems. Sexually I mean,' came the voice of his opponent.

Next ball just made it into the pocket.

'Still, at your age these things happen, especially without the right partner,' came that voice again.

The pink ball had a tremendous difficulty finding the pocket.

All down to a black ball game. Jacob, as ever, took his time.

So, for once, did Bo. Waited for quite a while.

As Jacob went to pot the black, Bo dealt his final stroke.

'Strelka is five months' pregnant and we'd like your opinion on what to name our child.'

Jacob's cue ripped the baize cloth.

And then it was on for young and old. By the time the police had dragged the two main protagonists apart, Jacob had a broken nose while Bo's left eye was closed completely.

So ended the Great South Bristol Snooker Game.

The rest is history. Jacob and Bo were banned for life from the snooker hall. Both Marynia and Strelka welcomed the decision. (Some say they were responsible for it in the first place.)

Jacob departed the South Bristol scene shortly afterwards. Strelka did not.

The divorce came through some years later, and Bo and Strelka's marriage took place shortly afterwards. It was a great occasion, but not unexpected.

Strelka is now a very contented mother. Marynia dotes on her grandson. Only contention is what his name should be. But that's the trouble with Central European families. Three people, five different opinions.

Bo has his own private opinion. Kid should be called Bohdan. Because that's what he is – a gift from God. And Bo's already working on that sawn-off snooker cue.

Ned

They buried Ned the day before Christmas Eve. I had hoped to be at the ceremony but business reasons made it impossible for me to attend. But I was there in spirit. Wishing, hoping he'd find a better life after this one.

I had only known the old fella for ten years. But those fortnightly visits stay in my mind. Someone without a bad thing to say about anybody, someone who would listen to all your problems, and whether or not he could help, at least he gave that reassuring touch.

The children in the neighbourhood doted on him. He was a devoted friend; someone to turn to in times of trouble. Never failed anyone who needed him. A mate to play with, a guardian, but most of all, someone who really cared. Not many like him around these days.

I knew there was something wrong with him some time ago. Old age brings its usual collection of problems. First the deafness. Then the arthritis. And finally the tumours that seem to spawn like Satan's weeds.

We all hoped he'd somehow get better. Each time I saw him, I'd try to buck him up a bit, tell him things were going to get better. But he let me know in his own silent way that he knew his best days were past, and all he hoped for now was a dignified exit from this life.

I went to his grave just the other day, to pay my respects to a true gentleman. His family had done him proud. A small plot, beautifully cared for, with bush rock borders and a native Australian bush plant already beginning to burgeon. A fitting place for one of this country's unsung heroes.

They award medals to people on the New Year's Honours List who may deserve them. I cannot comment on that as I do not know any of the recipients, or their contribution to society. That is decided by powers higher than I can aspire to. But as far as I'm concerned, Ned has a medal in my heart. And he deserved it better than most.

Epilogue

Ned was a family dog, an English boxer to be exact. To me, and to his family, he was one of us, and a true and loyal friend.

Hope and pray there really is that big kennel in the sky.

The Eagle and the Falcon

I met him in the May of 1994, in the Polish Club in Ashfield, Sydney, Australia. The exact date was 24 May, though I did not realise the significance of that at the time. Just an old man sitting on his own, wearing a black beret and clothes that had known better days.

What intrigued me was that in front of him was a small bottle of Polish vodka, two glasses, and a small bunch of flowers – two red-and-white carnations, some blue irises, and two yellow daffodils.

I'd had a good day at the races and, being naturally gregarious, thought I would have some words with the old gentleman, perhaps buy him a drink and ask him the significance of the flowers in particular and also the empty glass. He accepted. And so unfolded the story.

His name was Mirek. Born in Lwów, which, in 1939, was a part of eastern Poland, but now is one of the main cities of the Ukraine. Fiercely patriotic, he had volunteered for army service in the late thirties and spent most of the time with the border guards on the Russian border. He was due to be demobbed a few weeks before the war began. The German invasion put paid to that.

I noticed the white eagle he had pinned on his lapel. Yes, he said, part of my old uniform, kept it with me all those years during the war and after, a reminder of my home country.

Mirek was wounded in the last week of September 1939 near the now completely unknown village of Piwlice during the final German assault. The bullet had gone clean through his leg. Despite suffering serious blood loss, he was nevertheless able to crawl away from the advancing Germans towards the eastern border.

He crawled for three days. The local villagers were so terrified of the oncoming Germans that not many were able, or dared, to help a wounded Polish soldier, an act that could have led to their own swift demise. He was desperate. At one stage, he even traded his army boots for half a loaf of bread and a bowl of soup. But he survived. And the hate grew. Hate for the Germans who had invaded his country; hate for his own countrymen who would not help him.

Then the Russians came and he became a prisoner of war. Initially he was more than grateful for the medical help and assistance that they provided. Only later did the interrogations begin, and the indoctrination that led to a situation for which, to this day, he hated the regime that caused it. More hate and bitterness.

It was around this time he met Dimitri Sokolniuk, who, though Ukrainian by birth, had also enlisted in the Polish Army. Like Mirek, Dimitri had been wounded in those last days of the September campaign. Dimitri was also fiercely patriotic – his loyalty belonging more to the Ukraine than to Poland.

Though hospitalised in adjoining beds, the pair never hit it off. For some reason, there was an immediate antipathy between the two men. Dimitri was a peasant farmer from the depths of Ruthenia; Mirek, a teacher by profession, thought himself superior.

In those days, there was violent animosity between Poles and Ukrainians, animosity which frequently translated into theft, murder, rape and other atrocities. Given this situation, it seemed perfectly normal to Mirek to begin to hate Dimitri, a feeling he was sure was reciprocated.

While both were in the same harsh circumstances, neither would raise a finger to help the other. Each kept himself to himself, delighting in the fact when the other was undergoing a particularly hard time.

But Fate, being the cruel mistress that she is, ensured that, after their period of convalescence when all captured Polish troops were packed off to Siberia, Mirek and Dimitri ended up in the same shipment. There followed years of malnutrition, severe hard labour, relentless bitter cold and the feeling of utter despair when it seemed that neither would see their beloved country again.

But that did not stop the feud between Mirek and Dimitri. They fought over scraps of food. They accused each other of unsoldierly conduct, stealing, black marketeering… anything that came to mind.

Then came the day when it was announced that a Polish Army force was being recruited on Soviet territory to join the Allied Forces in the Middle East. Mirek's eyes filled with tears as he described the initial address by their commander, Lieutenant General Anders, to that ragged, hopeless band of men in the wilds of Siberia.

Apparently, one word did it. Anders started off his speech with the word 'Soldiers'. Mirek said the effect was miraculous. Suddenly that rag-tag bunch of prisoners was transformed – shoulders straightened, chests were pushed out, they all felt they were men again. And not just men, but soldiers. Polish soldiers.

Except, as far as Mirek was concerned, Dimitri. But what could you expect from a Ukrainian peasant? He would probably desert at the first opportunity. God, how he hated him.

So the journey began. Packed into cattle trucks, men, women and children made that epic journey from Russia, through Iran and on to the Middle East. All driven by the hope that, at last, life could start again. There would be a chance of freedom, and yes, revenge.

Of course, this had nothing to do with the private war between Mirek and Dimitri. When the carriage they were travelling in caught fire and the resultant emergency stop caused Mirek to fall heavily, losing most of his teeth in the process, Dimitri just smiled and looked the other way. Similarly, when Dimitri badly scalded his hand, all Mirek would offer was, 'You should be more careful.'

It was in this happy state of affairs that they finally arrived in Libya. There, the army training was resumed. Apart from anything else, they all had to learn to deal with new equipment, new regulations, a new (British) way of conducting a war.

Mirek was reinstated to his old rank of corporal, while Dimitri remained, as ever, a private. This naturally gave rise to even greater animosity between the two men. Dimitri would delight in carrying out Mirek's orders in the longest time possible, while Mirek used all in his power to make Dimitri's life hell.

A typical example occurred one hot day. Mirek ordered Dimitri to fetch some water for the platoon. Dimitri ambled over to the water cart, filled the necessary water bottles, and made his equally slow way back. Just to drive home the point, he turned 180 degrees and stopped, as if fascinated by the sight of something in the desert in front of him.

It was at this precise moment that an army jeep came hurtling round the corner heading straight for Dimitri. It was only the split-second reflexes of Mirek, who flung himself forward in a textbook rugby tackle, that prevented a potentially fatal incident.

Time for expressions of gratefulness, thanks, relief that no harm had been done? Not a bit of it. This was a time for retribution. Mirek accused Dimitri of negligence and insubordination, while Dimitri responded by threatening to have Mirek charged with assaulting a member of the lower ranks. Aspersions were cast on the paternity of each participant by the other, likewise the maternal morality of the ones who gave them birth.

It was in this spirit of mutual dislike, bordering on hatred, that they found themselves with the Polish II Corps of the British Eighth Army on the slopes of Monte Cassino in southern Italy in May 1944.

The battle for Monte Cassino has been described as arguably the toughest, hardest, most vicious campaign in the Western theatre of World War II operations. Even today, a visit to the site cannot fail to bring tears to the eyes of anyone fortunate enough to experience it. The ruggedness of the terrain, the scenic beauty, and overriding it all the thought of the young men who died and whose graves can still be seen there are enough to stir the most cynical of hearts.

The Polish involvement lasted just two weeks, at a cost of over 1,000 lives.

Mirek's and Dimitri's involvement was just slightly less.

Mirek had asked for the transfer of his fractious subordinate in the days preceding the first attack. No way, he was told. This was not the time to be moving people around for personal reasons. So, once again, they had to adapt.

The initial attack saw them cut to pieces on Phantom Ridge and left the platoon decimated. The second one was no better. But through it all Mirek and Dimitri continued to argue about who did the wrong thing at the right time or vice versa.

Came the night of 24 May 1944. They'd been told this was the last assault, the final attempt to take Monte Cassino. Basically, do or die. For Mirek, this was the opportunity to unleash all the hate and bitterness of the last five years. All he wanted to do was to kill, to mutilate, to destroy, to get his revenge.

The remnants of the platoon were embedded on the slopes of Monte San Angelo. From where he was, Mirek could see the bombed-out ruins of the abbey across the valley. Between them was not just the valley, but also the terrifying prospect of the ascent to the peak of Monte Cassino itself. So near, and yet so far…

Minefields, snipers, bunkers, grenades, mortar, everything one could think of, the Germans had it ready for them. But this had to be done. The time had come for revenge. He looked at what was left of his platoon. Yes, they'll do their best, he thought. Every one of them, except for that bastard Dimitri. Surprised he's still with us, he thought. Must have the luck of the devil with him. With a bit of luck, he'll stop the first bullet.

The hate grew. He gave the signal for advance.

It happened so quickly his mind couldn't react. One explosion, overwhelming pain, and then nothing.

He awoke in a hospital bed. It took him a while to come to his senses. Then he called for the nurse. She called for the doctor.

The doctor was quite matter-of-fact. 'Don't worry, Corporal Sibierski, you'll make a full recovery. Unfortunately, we could not save your right leg. But they can do wonders with prosthetics these days; and a spell in the rehabilitation hospital is exactly what you need right now. And there's also the bonus that, for you, the war is over.'

'What about my platoon?'

'They were not so lucky,' came the grave reply. 'But you must have had a very loyal friend in that Ukrainian fellow, Sokolniuk, I believe his name was. Hit twice trying to carry you back to the medical post. Definitely saved your life. Unfortunately, just as he got there, the third bullet got him.'

Epilogue

Mirek wiped away some tears from his eyes.

'There is no point in harbouring hatred or bitterness, or looking for revenge,' he told me. 'All that does is eat away at you and make you a lesser person. Keep that in mind, young man, and remember always to value your friends.'

'That's why I come here every time on the twenty-fourth of May,' the old man said. 'To remember the best friend I never knew I had. Today is the fiftieth anniversary of his death. The empty glass is for him, the vodka is what I so much want to share with him but cannot, the red-and-white carnations are for the country we both fought for, and the blue and yellow flowers are for the one he carried in his heart.'

He finished his glass, shook my hand, picked up his cane and the flowers and slowly limped away.

Just another old man with a lot of memories and not one friend in this world.

The Match

Introduction

It was a match he had hoped he would never have to play. Even though it was rugby, a sport he loved above all others. But he could sense, feel, that there would be trouble involved: trouble he would rather not be part of; trouble he wanted to avoid at all costs. And he was quite right. There was.

The Early Days

His name was Mark Carroll. Eldest son of Sean and Maureen Carroll, Irish Catholics from County Mayo in the west of Ireland who emigrated in search of work and a better future for themselves and their family.

On arrival in their new country, they gravitated naturally towards their own – as so many migrants do. So Mark was brought up in a small Irish enclave in a working-class part of town.

Those early days were the happiest Mark could remember. A loving family and a host of young lads his age with whom he could share the discoveries of life. There was one bad period when he was diagnosed with tuberculosis – still fairly common in those days. He had to spend a few months in hospital. But even then his friends rallied round and when he was finally discharged life resumed its previous happy course.

Impromptu football games at the bottom of the cul-de-sac,

visits to the local swimming baths where each would dare the others to dive off the highest diving board, the first realisations that girls could be interesting.

Yes, he experienced it all. And even then, hoped it would never end. But life is not all a bed of roses, as the old cliché goes. As he was soon to find out.

The Middle Years

The education system in those days was heavily influenced by what was called the eleven-plus, an examination taken by students at roughly the age of eleven. Those who passed the examination were eligible to enter what was called a grammar school; those who did not were afforded places in what was then called a secondary modern, later, comprehensive school.

Mark was the only one of his circle of friends who passed the examination. Ended up with a scholarship at St Patrick's.

All the rest ended up at St Anne's.

And it was as if a barrier had suddenly sprung up between him and his old friends. Oh, they were polite enough to him, but gradually excluded him from their group, basically made him feel he was no longer part of things.

For the first time in his life he experienced loneliness – and he did not like it.

But youth is naturally resilient. Mark began to forge new relationships, making friends with lads from his new school environment. And he was successful to a point.

But somehow nothing seemed to be able to replace those days at the bottom of the cul-de-sac.

The Teenage Years

He did well at school. A good intelligence, a naturally friendly manner, both teamed with more than reasonable sporting abilities (probably inherited from his father) suggested this lad could go far.

He represented his school in athletics during the summer months and rugby during the winter. But rugby was his real interest. Before St Patrick's he'd never experienced the game. It was rarely played in the Ireland that he knew, where Gaelic football was the main sporting preoccupation during the winter months. And that first match made him an instant convert. St Patrick's lost the game, but only narrowly, to a side which included several over-age players. More to the point, Mark scored his first try. The feeling was indescribable, one he would relive over and over again.

Girls, especially one, seemed to feature more and more in his life. But he was still a young lad finding his way in life and realised there would be more of that to come later.

A couple of brushes with the law – nothing too serious, just what one might expect of a lad his age with a bit of the larrikin in him. Certainly nothing to cause his family any shame or aggravation. Mark set great store by that. He owed them too much to do anything else.

So overall, good days, filled with adventure, discovery, and promise of even better things to come.

But every now and again there would be that twinge of nostalgia for the days in that cul-de-sac. More than nostalgia – a sense of loss, of rejection.

The Problem

Damian Flynn was not a nice character. A teacher, who, at best, could be described as average and, at worst, a religious zealot par excellence. Mark found himself with Flynn as his teacher and rugby coach in the same year. The problem started right away.

St Patrick's had a tradition of fostering formal debates for its senior students. The topic on this particular day was 'How relevant is the Catholic Church in these times?'

Mark was assigned to state the case for the negative. And he did so, with a well-rehearsed and researched speech which covered everything from divorce to the right of women to abortion in certain circumstances.

He had barely started on the abortion issue when Damian Flynn intervened, crying out at the top of his voice, 'This is heresy!'

Mark just smiled that smile of his and said, softly, 'Sir, I believe you are labouring under a misconception.'

Brought the house down, but also the hope of any rational relationship between Mark and Damian Flynn.

The Training

Though a more than passable player in his day, Damian Flynn was not adept at passing those skills on to his charges. In fact, exactly the opposite.

Since the event of the debate, he made it a special point to belittle Mark's efforts on the rugby field regardless of the effect it would have on Mark's morale or the team's as a whole. He would ensure Mark did more than his fair share of training, denigrated his tackling skills, said he wasn't fit to wear the school colours. Only the intervention of the school Principal, to whose attention this had come, stopped him from dropping Mark from the team altogether. Fortunately, the Principal was also a devotee of rugby and was not going to lose someone he considered one of his best players.

Especially with the most important game of the season looming in sight. The one to decide the best team in town.

Against St Anne's.

Match Day

The rain had been torrential for the past twenty-four hours. It was still raining as the two teams prepared to take the field.

The reception Mark had received from the opposition when he arrived left him in no doubt what to expect. No quarter whatsoever. Time to put a certain someone in his place. They had been his friends, now he was their enemy.

He wished it could have been different.

He was picked to play on the left wing. Exactly why was a mystery, since he was naturally a right-footed player.

The ground sloped somewhat from left to right. The far right corner was the lowest part of the pitch.

St Patrick's lost the toss but, surprisingly, were allowed the use of the high ground in the first half if they wanted it. And so they did. And the rain kept falling.

First Half

Mark knew he was in for a torrid time straight from the kick-off. Damian Flynn's tactics were for his side to use the left or higher (therefore relatively drier) part of the ground. So he got more than his fair share of the ball. And more than his fair share of attention from St Anne's defence.

But he gritted his teeth and battled through. Till that magical moment ten minutes from the end of the first half when he received the ball, deftly side-stepped a defender, palmed off another one and set off down the touchline like a rabbit with a pack of greyhounds in pursuit, to score in the corner.

True to his make-up, Damian Flynn awarded the usual praise at half-time. Said the whole team was playing like five-year-olds and it was lucky they were ahead because, 'Carroll fluked that try even though he should have passed the ball to someone in a better position.' Said he expected a better effort in the second half.

Second Half

St Anne's tactics became clear from the first minute. Consisted of repeatedly kicking for the lowest corner of the field which by now had turned into the biggest mud bath God could have ever invented. Exactly the place where Mark formed the last line of defence.

Which he did for a long time. Up to his ankles in mud, tackling, pushing, shoving – anything to keep the other side out. But eventually they scored. The scores were now level and there were still ten minutes left. Mark could see the derisive smiles on the faces of his former friends as they prepared for the final assault.

'Not so smart now, are we?' was one of the nicer comments that came his way.

The Final Score

I wish I could tell you that Mark and his team held on, at least for an honourable draw. But in real life things do not happen like that.

With one minute to go St Anne's went in for the winning score. Their cheers could be heard all over town. All that Mark was left with was one completely closed eye, one missing tooth, multiple cuts to his face and body and a feeling that he had been run over by a herd of buffalo with steel-tipped hooves.

And a pang of longing for those days in the cul-de-sac.

The Aftermath

Damian Flynn was not one to hold back. He stormed across the field to where Mark was lying exhausted and bleeding on the ground and promptly let off a diatribe to the effect that Mark, and Mark alone, was responsible for St Patrick's defeat.

A short silence followed. Mark was too far gone to reply.

But the St Anne's captain could and did. If I remember correctly, the words were:

'You are talking about the best player on this field. The one who definitely did not deserve to be on the losing side. Who gave the best he could and then more. And what's more, you're slagging off a close friend of ours.'

With that most of the team picked up Damian Flynn bodily and deposited him face down in that very mud pile that Mark had been protecting for most of that game.

Epilogue

As far as I know, Mark is the only player ever to be chaired off the field by the opposing side.

Seems the spirit of the cul-de-sac had never really disappeared.

Chloe

I saw her for the first time today. One of those magic moments in life when you fall in love all over again.

Her parents are Martin and Mary, from one of the less fashionable suburbs of western Sydney, NSW, Australia. They're people who, in our part of the world, we call battlers – hard-pressed to make ends meet while struggling to exist with dignity and give their children the best chance in life that they can, in circumstances that most people better off would find hard to imagine.

Mary is a nurse working mainly the night shifts. The pay is better than for day work and the arrangement gives her the chance to be with their children during most of the day. Martin basically turns his hand to whatever he can. And it means that he can care for the children while Mary is at work. It's a reasonable arrangement and between them they manage to get by without being a drain on the government's purse.

Martin had been married before, so brought to the union with Mary a daughter from that past. They had another daughter before Chloe. So that makes three girls in all, including Chloe.

But to me Chloe was something special.

I was doing some work for them one day and had my eighteen-year-old son with me to lend a hand. I realised that Mary was very proud of her daughter, but very protective towards her and quite rightly so. So I warned my son to watch his step and behave with all the necessary decorum. Probably just as well. My son is very fond of the fair sex and can be, let us say, somewhat forward at times.

But I was the one who saw her first and was absolutely smitten.

I think it was her lovely face, small delicate hands and that air of vulnerability that made my heart go out to her. And I had no compunction about telling her so.

I also told her parents. They had no objections, in fact quite the opposite. After all, I was a well known and respected member of the community and they had dealt with me many times before. So it would be fair to say that they trusted me. I, for my part, would never do anything to break that trust.

Mary called me in so I could meet her daughter and, like I said, I was totally smitten. I was able to speak with her, but the time for me to depart came all too quickly. Leaving her was like losing a part of myself.

Before the work was finished, my young son also made her acquaintance. This was definitely not my idea. I would have preferred to have had her all to myself. But Martin and Mary insisted.

My son also fell in love with her straight away. But that's youth for you, totally impulsive.

We left shortly after, with the promise that we would visit again soon. Both Martin and Mary said they hoped that time would not be too long away. They were sure that Chloe would agree.

As I mentioned before, these are two special people, whose love and dedication to their children no one could question.

All the way home my son and I argued whom Chloe had liked the best. In the end we settled for an honourable draw. But we both want to see her again.

Epilogue

Chloe was twelve weeks old today.

To me she is a reminder of the wonder I felt when my son was born and I first held him in my arms and experienced the love flow from me to him. That is a memory which will live for ever in my heart.

To my son, I hope it is a fitting reminder of how precious young babies can be and the responsibility each parent takes on when they create one. Maybe, just maybe, it will teach him something about life. Ever the optimist, I truly believe it will.

To Martin and Mary, Chloe is just a treasure.

Neighbours
(or The Dogs' Dunny)

Introduction

A good neighbour can be one of the best things this world has to offer. Someone ready to help in times of need; someone for whom you would do exactly the same with pleasure; someone with whom to share life's joys or troubles.

In other words, a friend.

Unfortunately there is another kind of neighbour. The sort who seems hell-bent on making community life as difficult as possible. The sort that will exploit every opportunity to advance a private point, gain some sort of perceived advantage, as if life was a contest rather than a pleasant experience.

I've known both types. One of them I treasure; the other, well, let's just say I don't. You be the judge.

Background

The house that I had built was on a sloping block. Sloping downwards to the rear.

The original owner of the house behind mine was a real knockabout character with whom I shared many a drink and friendly conversation. He looked after my dog when I was at work, and I helped him to find his when the bitch went AWOL, usually when on heat.

So life was quite pleasant until the day when he remarried and his new wife wanted to move elsewhere. And when he sold the house. And when the new neighbour moved in.

The troubles began almost immediately.

First there were the complaints that rain run-off from my block was doing damage to his backyard. I pointed out that:

a) I had not caused it to rain in the first place;

b) there was no way, short of divine intervention, that I could make rainwater run uphill; and

c) what the hell did he expect from buying a house on the wrong end of a downward slope?

That seemed to settle things for a while, though mysterious lumps of mud began to occasionally appear on my side of the fence, coincidentally just after a heavy rainfall. I kept my mouth shut.

This was closely followed by broken tree branches. Admittedly the trees were on my property and he was quite within his rights to throw them over for me to dispose of. On the other hand, it would have been just as easy to put them out with all the rest of the recyclable garden stuff for the Council to pick up as they usually did on a fortnightly basis.

Still, I kept my mouth shut.

The main problem featured the dogs.

By now I had two of them, both kelpies, good watchdogs, who'd bark if any unknown person appeared on the property. Just doing their job.

The hate mail began to arrive. Anonymous, of course. Advising me of measures that would be taken if I could not control my fierce animals.

By this time I had a fair idea who was orchestrating this campaign so off I went to confront my neighbour. I probably should not have bothered. He denied any involvement.

The next stage involved the local council ranger, who appeared one day to check complaints that I was mistreating my dogs. I showed her the dogs, the conditions they were kept in, vaccination certificates, etc. She was more than satisfied.

So I asked her who had filed the complaint. She said that council policy prevented her from doing that.

'That's a pity,' I said. 'But it obviously has to be someone local. I bet you could see the place from here.'

She smiled, and looked straight at my neighbour's house.

That was enough for me. But, as she said that the complaint would be rejected and the complainant notified, I kept my mouth shut.

And life moved on.

The Dogs' Dunny

As I said, by this time I had two dogs. The only trouble with that is that dogs tend to relieve themselves in all sorts of places and I have yet to find one who can be trained to use a toilet. This leaves the owner with the responsibility of disposing of the waste in a reasonable manner.

The toilet is one way, a plastic bag in the weekly rubbish is another.

But you're talking to an Aussie, with far more ingenious ideas than normal in most other places in the world.

I discovered there was this thing best described as a dogs' dunny: a large PVC container which could be buried in a gravel or rubble pit in the garden, then filled with water up to the level where an outlet pipe allowed excess to flow away.

Into this dunny would be fed all the dogs' excreta and with the addition of some enzyme pellets would cause non-toxic, positively environmentally-friendly liquid to leach into the garden and help beautify this wonderful suburb of mine.

Unfortunately, I got the first attempt slightly wrong. In my haste, I did not allow for sufficient rubble or gravel.

The result was entirely predictable.

The whole thing clogged up.

So I was faced with the prospect of digging the whole thing up again and replacing it in a more proper setting.

Now, I don't know if you have ever tried to relocate a binful of dog excreta. If you haven't, my advice would be not to bother.

By the time my son and I finished the exercise, taken umpteen showers and used enough deodorant to send the chemical stocks on the Stock Exchange into the stratosphere, we were still so heavy on the nose that we had to eat by ourselves for the next two weeks.

But hope springs eternal. So, not too long afterwards, the Dogs' Dunny No. 2 Project began, this time done with meticulous care – we did not want a repeat of the other episode.

And who should surface except our old friend, the neighbour. Stuck his face over the fence and asked what we were doing. I explained to him the benefits of the undertaking and how it would benefit local ecology.

He seemed to accept it.

Till I got a letter from the local council telling me there was a complaint from a local resident that I was installing a septic toilet in a sewered area and would I remove it before they took legal action.

Like before, I kept my mouth shut and got ready to dismantle the dogs' dunny all over again.

But I did have a word with my son.

A Slight Diversion

Now, my son is not a bad looker – has more than the average amount of charm. I like to think he gets it from me, but who knows?

My neighbour has a daughter. Quite nice, despite her parentage.

The Finale

There I am, digging up the dogs' dunny again. Up pops this face over the fence. Says it should never have happened in the first place.

I keep my mouth shut.

Asks me where my loyal assistant – i.e. son – is and why he's not helping out with the job.

This time I do not keep my mouth shut.

Tell him his daughter has designs on my son and the last I heard they were off to some local park for a spot of *al fresco amore*.

Never seen a bloke move so fast in my life.

Trouble is, there are quite a few parks in this area.

And my son and his daughter are not in any of them.

I know exactly where they are. In fact, I gave them the keys.

In the meantime, I'll get on with digging out this dogs' dunny.

But now the skies seem bluer, the sun is shining, the birds are singing and I believe I can smell roses in the air.

The Honeymoon

Introduction

For 99% of the population, the first day of their honeymoon is the happiest one in their life. There's the promise of delights to come, disaffection and problems are still over the horizon, and there's the prospect of spending the next two weeks alone with the one you love, and who loves you more than anything else in the world.

Then there is the other 1%. I believe I fitted into that category.

Background

I remember waking up that morning with a severe hangover and a feeling that something serious and not very nice had happened the day before. It's well known to those of us who, on occasion, have over-imbibed the night before. I racked my brains for a few minutes. No, it wouldn't come to me. The hangover was too strong.

I turned over in the bed.

And suddenly the truth hit me like a sledgehammer.

I had also found the quickest cure for a hangover since man was first tempted to partake of some fermented brew or other.

I was married.

I looked across to where she lay – cold cream on her face,

curlers in her hair, mouth open as she snored gently.

What on earth had possessed me?

I had planned to get out of this particular impediment, but family pressures and a misguided sense of honour finally made me go through with it.

So here I was. Married when I did not want to be, about to embark on this honeymoon I would have rather preferred to skip altogether and the plane was due to take off shortly. With a heavy heart I packed a suitcase and prepared for the great 'adventure'.

The Events

We boarded the plane at Heathrow and jetted off for Kérkira, or Corfu as it's more commonly known.

Ten minutes into the flight my wife became violently air-sick. She stayed that way for the full three hours of the journey. At this stage my contribution was to pass full airsick bags to the stewardess while fortifying myself with a steady supply of gin and tonics.

By God, I was feeling better by the minute. Pausing only to offer the odd throwaway line of false sympathy I worked my way through most of a bottle of gin.

We finally landed in Corfu. The wife assured me she would now be OK since we were on firm ground.

Pity, thought I. I had rather enjoyed the absence of sound from her, apart from the occasional heave as she filled up yet another airsick bag.

What no one had told us, however, was that the airport was at the north end of the island and the hotel at the south end – another journey of three hours, this time by bus.

The wife now became violently carsick.

The lovely young lady whose responsibility it was to look after the bus passengers became increasingly frazzled at the procession of sick bags, while I marvelled how my wife could still have anything left in her stomach.

But I'm a resilient person and I did have a bottle of duty-free vodka on my person, which helped to while away the time. And all the time there was this blessed (almost) silence. So it was with mixed feelings on my part that we finally arrived at the hotel.

The management knew we were a honeymoon couple, so in the room were a bowl of fruit, some flowers and a bottle of champagne. The wife promptly passed out in bed, her final words being that she was exhausted and did not want to be disturbed.

This left me to my own devices, which suited me just fine. The flowers and fruit were consigned to some dark recess of the room. Not so the champagne. Oh no.

This was promptly consumed by yours truly, and very nice it was too. Then I ventured out to see what Corfu had to offer.

Not much, it seemed.

We were at the southern, least populated part of the island. The hotel had very little in the way of entertainment at that time of evening but I was assured there was a very nice taverna just across the small river at the back of the hotel.

'How does one get across the river?' I asked.

Apparently there was a boat (I am being generous with that description) with a steel cable leading to the opposite bank. By cranking up the winch, the cable moved the boat which steadily made its way to the other side. As it happened a few people were heading across as well so I did not have to exert myself on this particular occasion. Probably just as well. The full force of the champagne and vodka, plus the gin and tonics, was finally kicking in.

Landing on the other side I found there were two tavernas, not one. No problem. I resolved to share my time equally between them.

I started off in the time-honoured way with some beer. But

it wasn't long before I was persuaded by the locals to try 'ouzo', the local firewater. 'But drink it with water,' they urged.

Now I felt that this cast aspersions on my manhood so I proceeded to drink it neat. Quite a lot of it, really, washing down the souvlaki with chips that seemed to materialise out of nowhere.

My confidence was growing by the minute. I was determined to show these Greeks what a real man could do.

I headed off for the second taverna.

There the welcome was even more rapturous than in the first one. Obviously the news of my coming had spread like wildfire through the small village and everyone wanted to see this eccentric Anglo who had stumbled into their midst.

This time I had a bottle of retsina thrust at me. I was feeling fine, so I gladly accepted it and polished it off. Another one materialised.

Then the Greek dancing started. To those of you unfamiliar with this aspect of culture, the men dance by themselves, women being confined to the sidelines where their expected contribution is to make the appropriate sounds of awe at the grace and ability of the dancers. A very enlightened race, the Greeks.

Apart from an initial misunderstanding when a burly Greek seemed to be getting a little bit too familiar for comfort, I thought I made more than a reasonable job of it. In fact, I was sure I did. I dipped and swayed with the best of them. I could see I had impressed the audience because they kept on pointing me out to each other and it was obvious I'd brought them happiness by the loud laughs and thigh-slapping which greeted some of my more skilful moves.

But all good things eventually have to come to an end. My watch seemed to have gone funny – it could not have been as late as that, after all, I'd only been there a few minutes – but I thought this might be an appropriate time to head home. So, pausing only for half an hour to drink some Metaxa brandy with my newfound friends, I reluctantly turned for home.

Up until now the day had turned out rather well.

The Boat

I arrived at the little river to see no sign of the boat on which I had come over. It appears they take it away somewhere after a certain time in the middle of the night.

Selfish lot.

I looked up and down the riverbank to see what else was available. Luckily enough I came across another boat, albeit a bit rough-looking, but good enough, I reckoned, to get me to the other side.

Now those of you who have been following this story closely may have noticed that, although by nature abstemious, by now I'd had a tiny bit more to drink than perhaps I should have had. This may go some way to explaining what happened next.

The boat was virtually identical to the one I had come across in, with the same winch mechanism, which I proceeded to crank up. Off I went across the little river. There was but one fundamental difference between the two boats. The other one had flooring. Large sections were missing in this one. I would have noticed this in a sober state, but what with the darkness and everything…

About one third of the way across I realised there was something wrong because the water was lapping at my feet. But it was too late to turn back so I cranked the winch harder and refused to think of the hundreds of marine accidents that happen every day.

At the halfway point the water was up to my waist and I was doing a more than passable impersonation of the captain of the Titanic. Only thing I needed was a band playing 'Abide With Me'.

I decided to swim for the far shore. Now this is not quite as easy as you may think, especially when one is in full dress and inebriated to boot. But never let it be said that members of my family give up in the face of adversity. While the stroke would not have won a medal at the Olympics, it got me across.

So there I was, minus one shoe, on the other side. But the gods had not finished with me yet.

The little river was a tidal one. At this particular stage the tide was out. This meant that instead of just sliding on to the grass I would have to scale the bank which at the moment bore a strong resemblance to the heights of Gallipoli or Quebec. Moreover, they consisted of pure, unadulterated, malodorous mud.

I will not bore you with the details. Suffice to say it took six attempts to scale that bank. Even General Wolfe at the Battle of Quebec did it quicker. At one stage I did think of just taking up a foetal position and hoping and praying that some passing shepherd would hear my lonely cries.

But even in Corfu the nights can be quite cold, especially if one is drenched to the skin, and philanthropic shepherds are hard to find. So I persevered and, finally, there was that blessed moment where I made it to the top.

The Aftermath

I realised that threading my way through the guests in the hotel might be somewhat problematic. It would not be that often that they get confronted with what looks like the Creature from the Black Lagoon.

As it turned out, when I squelched my way into the foyer, the first thing that happened is that I was confronted by the sight of my wife pleading with the manager to call out the police, the militia, the dog squad, *anyone* who could trace my whereabouts. The epitome of a distraught wife.

When she saw me her mood rapidly changed. While a pool of water gradually increased around my feet, spoiling what had been rather a fetching carpet, she let me know precisely how long she had been worrying and how furious she was.

'Well,' she shrieked, finally, 'what are you going to about it?'

That was an easy one.

'Frankly, sweetheart,' I said, in what I hoped was a passable imitation of Clark Gable, 'I'm going to take a shower. Then I'll put on some dry clothes. After that I'll find a bar that is open. It's been a stressful day. Not all of us can afford the luxury of sleeping it all away. So you'll forgive me when I say I don't give a damn.'

She didn't.

I won't tell you what she said. Even in these enlightened times certain words and phrases are considered unprintable.

The marriage did not last too long after that. Personally, I blame it all on the demon drink. But I'm the eternal optimist: if it had not been for the drink, I might still be married today. Not a happy thought.

The Orange and the Green
(or, the wildness breaks out through the
eyes of a cat)

Introduction

They were probably the most ill assorted couple you could ever find, at least in the Ireland of 1969. A pair of star-crossed lovers if ever I saw one. Doubt if anyone would have given them a chance especially with their ill-fated beginning. I know, because I was there.

Kevin

His full name was Kevin Michael Maguire, originally from County Cork. His father, Padraic Maguire, had him baptised so in honour of two of the Republic's legends – Kevin Barry, who became a martyr to the Republican cause when hanged by the British in Mountjoy Jail; and Michael Collins, who so effectively led the IRA in the years following the 1916 Easter Rising and eventually brought about the birth of the Irish Free State. Before, as has been the tragedy of Ireland throughout the centuries, being assassinated by a fellow countryman in West Cork on the grounds that he gave in too much to the British and allowed them to keep the Six Counties in the north.

Padraic was one of Collins' flying brigade. A very hard man indeed. He had seen his family home burnt down by the Black and Tans, and a brother killed for no better reason than that he bore the same surname. He was not a man to forgive and forget. People still remember that one gaze from those steely blue eyes was enough to put the fear of the Lord into anyone who crossed his path. For a number of Black and Tans and their informers, that was the last thing they ever saw.

Kevin grew up in that sort of atmosphere, surrounded by that sort of history. And imbued with the passion it generated. The only mediating force was his mother, Mary, who tried to teach him that hate was no reason for existence. Some of that advice had an impact on the lad, but only some.

Some, but I'll describe that later. Again, I know because I was there to see it.

Mary

Born Mary McTaggart, daughter of a worker at the shipyards in Belfast. Obviously a Protestant and Loyalist, because they did not employ too many Catholics or Nationalists at those shipyards.

She was imbued with the Loyalist traditions, taught that the Republicans were the scum of the earth, leeching on the good-will and generosity of the hard-working Protestant community. In her sheltered world she had no reason to doubt that reasoning. After all, her whole family adopted it. All the same, her intuitive female feelings gnawed away, saying, 'Mary, this is not how life should be.'

But in the sectarian world of Belfast, there really was no one to turn to for advice or guidance. So she learned to put up with the bigotry and hatred she heard day after day. Still, she lived in the hope that somewhere there was a better world and somehow she would be fortunate to eventually live there and, more importantly, the right person with whom she could share that dream.

In the meantime, life went on. Every 12 July she'd witness the parades that commemorated some long-forgotten battle and brought out the worst in people. She yearned for a life without bitterness and hate, a life with someone caring and thoughtful, who'd love her for what she was, not for some political ideal.

I only found out about this later, but, as I say, I was a witness to all of it. And when I did my heart went out to the girl.

And I was glad when she finally confided in me.

Kevin and Mary

It was not an auspicious start. Mary was a waitress in a café in one of the so-called neutral areas of the city. She'd noticed before the dark-skinned young man with the curly black hair, the blue eyes and slightly shy manner. Hard not to. He was there every day.

Something drew her to him. In a lot of ways he was the person she had dreamed of. Caring and gentle. But there was something, some inner sense that told her, 'Be careful, this man could be dangerous. There is something hidden there.'

She noticed his left hand was scarred to the point of uselessness. She wanted to ask him how that had happened, but being a naturally shy person she could not bring herself to do it. I could have told her, but she did not ask.

'And a good morning to ye,' were the first words she heard that day. 'The name is Kevin Maguire and you're a sight for sore eyes on a morning such as this. I'll have a cup of tea and whatever else is going if that's all right by you.'

The sound of the County Cork accent immediately put her on her guard. Good God, she thought, he's from the South; bound to be a Catholic and a Nationalist as well. What would my family say if they saw me talking to him?

'Never saw such pretty red hair before in my life,' were the next words she heard. 'Goes well with those hazel eyes.'

The hazel eyes glazed over.

I'll have to get rid of him, she admonished herself. Yet

there's something there that draws me to him. Perhaps in a minute or two.

'And what should I be calling ye?' came that voice again.

'Mary,' she whispered, before realising what she had done.

'That's a grand auld name. Same as my mother's,' the inexorable voice went on. 'And what would you be doing this Saturday night?'

At this moment, anything for you, was her immediate reaction. But the words that came out were different. 'Getting ready for Sunday services, that's what. And you could do the same, you Papist bastard.'

The minute the words left her lips, she regretted them. But a word once said is like an arrow sped – no chance of calling it back.

He smiled, a trifle sadly. 'Then perhaps I'll see you one of these days. You take care, now.' With that he picked up his change and walked out of the door, just as she was about to tell him not to go, that she wanted to get to know him better, how much he already meant to her even after that short exchange.

I know how she felt, because I saw her cry.

Kevin

He had come up north to look for a job. He'd tried Strabane and Derry but there was not much going there. So he moved on to Belfast.

Times were not much better there either. But with the help of a few contacts, he finally got a job at the shipyard. Nothing much, just labouring, but the money would help with the rent.

Only trouble was that the job did not last very long. Southerners were not appreciated in the shipyards. Regarded as taking away the jobs of hard-working Orangemen with families to feed.

So what followed was inevitable. On the first day, he heard a shout of, 'Hey, Paddy, catch this!' He turned and caught the object thrown at him with his left hand. It was an iron bolt, white hot from the furnace.

So Kevin's shipbuilding career came to an end.

I was sorry to see it happen and felt guilty because I had been one of the prime movers in getting the job for him in the first place.

Mary

She cooked the evening meal for the family. Sat and listened to her father and brothers swapping the stories about football, snooker and manly exploits in the local pub.

She was not impressed. Surely there must be more to life than this? she thought.

Depends on one's point of view. The conversation had turned to work in the shipyards. To great guffaws of laughter, her father recounted a practical joke he'd played on some Southerner one day which had left him in the hospital emergency ward. 'Serves him right for trying to steal one of our jobs.' She hurried out of the room.

Kevin

Somewhat surprisingly, given his background, Kevin was not a Nationalist militant in any way.

He was a nationalist in the sense that he believed in a free and united Ireland, but his belief was that this could be achieved by means of the ballot box rather than rifles or bombs. He'd come to the attention of what was euphemistically known as 'the organisation', but quickly let it be known that he was not interested. Those who found it difficult to reconcile themselves with these notions and attempted to take the matter further soon found out that he was not a man to be trifled with, and after a short time all approaches ceased.

It would have probably stayed like that except for a twist of history.

Kevin was in Belfast when the Troubles started in 1969. When the Loyalist paramilitaries spilled out onto those hate-filled streets. When, for the Nationalist minority, the IRA seemed like the only hope for survival.

He joined up with one of the brigades straight away, and was involved in most of the action that followed.

He reminded me so much of his father in those days – same steely look, same ruthlessness, same impetuosity. There's a saying in Ireland: 'The wildness breaks out in the eyes of the cat.' He was his father's son, no doubt about that. And I was sad, in a way, to see those traits were used for motives we now prefer to forget.

But I also saw the caring and gentle side of the boy. Someone who would risk his life to help others, someone who comforted grieving families and helped them restore some normality to their lives.

Oh yes, I saw it all.

Mary

Of course, she knew about the violence. Everyone in Belfast did. She saw her father and brothers join the Loyalist para-militaries, saw them go out at night with rifles in their hands. Hoped and prayed they would still be there the following morning. They were her family, after all.

But increasingly her thoughts focused on Kevin. Because her intuition told her he was involved in this somewhere as well.

'God, please look after him and keep him safe,' became her daily prayer.

Kevin and Mary

Eighteen months had passed. The violence was still there, but more localised, more impersonal. In parts of the city, life returned to what could almost be described as normal.

She was still working in the same café as before. She heard the bell as the front door opened.

'And a fine good morning to you, Mary,' came a voice she immediately recognised. 'I'll be having a cup of tea, if it's not too much trouble.'

Yes. It was him again. Same look, same smile, just a small scar on his left cheek played witness to what had happened in the intervening time. She felt herself go weak at the knees, had to reach out to steady herself.

'That offer of Saturday night is still available,' came that voice. 'And I'd be honoured if you'd accept.'

This time there was no hesitation.

I was delighted, because in my mind these two young people deserved each other. And I was pleased to be there to witness it.

Epilogue

The saying about the IRA is, 'Once in, always in.' And they do not like deserters. Added to that was the fact that mixed marriages were not so much looked down on as abhorred in the province in those days – by both sides. Life looked very bleak for Kevin and Mary, despite their overwhelming love for each other.

But love will always find a way. And our twosome eventually found themselves on a plane bound for Australia under that country's plan for resettlement for special hardship cases.

I was there at the airport to see them off and wish them every happiness.

I was also there to welcome them back when the Troubles had eased and the IRA had granted an amnesty to all former members.

Only this time it was no longer just Kevin and Mary. There were four children in tow, two girls and two boys.

'Two Orange and two Green,' Kevin confided to me.

'Except we don't know which ones are which,' added Mary, 'and quite frankly we don't care.'

I agreed with the sentiments wholeheartedly.

Me

You may wonder who I am and how I've been so implicated in the lives of these people. I am a County Cork man myself and knew Kevin's mother and father well. Kevin's arrival in Belfast roughly coincided with mine. I followed his development with an uncle's interest. Because his uncle is who I am. Mary I met purely fortuitously, but am extremely happy that I did and that I helped these two in some small way to achieve happiness.

And I am extremely glad that the wildness no longer breaks out in the eyes of the cat as far as Kevin is concerned. I know Mary feels the same. The ghosts have been laid to rest.

I was primarily responsible for their emigration to Australia, and their eventual return.

How? I hear you ask.

Because I'm Chief of Staff of the IRA Belfast Brigades, is how.

The Dentist

Introduction

There is fairly large body of people out there in this fair world of ours who are, as far as I am concerned, legalised sadists. They are helped in their nefarious deeds by assistant sadists.

I refer, of course, to dentists and their nurses or receptionists, call them what you will.

Background

I first came across this species at a very young and impressionable age. In those days, of course, there was no such thing as local anaesthetic and gas was only used when major surgery was involved.

Anything else you had to put up with and never mind the pain. To this day, the sound of a dentist's drill is enough to reduce me to jelly.

Which is why I avoid these sadists as much as I can except in cases of extreme emergency.

I had managed reasonably well until a couple of years ago when a really bad toothache kept me up all night on Christmas Day and forced me to try to find a dentist on Boxing Day. There were only a few operating that day, but I was desperate.

This is when I first came across the resident sadist.

My worst fears were realised.

The injections were painful. More to the point, they seemed to take overly long to take effect. Which probably explains why, when the drill came into contact with my tooth, the resultant pain was enough to send me rocketing out of the chair.

The sadist did not seem fazed at all by this, but there again it wasn't him having his nerve-ends tickled by some mechanical monstrosity. He merely clucked a few times, said the task needed more anaesthetic, and promptly shoved another couple of needles into my defenceless gums.

With that, he was ready to carry on from where he was before. I, on the other hand, was not.

It was only the reminder of the pain I had been in the previous night that persuaded me to allow him to start again.

But the damage was done. Any chance of a rapprochement had disappeared for ever, much like my soon-to-be extracted teeth.

In fact, two teeth were extracted, and some cleaning and scraping took place until I begged him to stop. I was charged a fortune for the privilege, and then discharged on the proviso that I return in the next two weeks for more remedial work.

Small chance, I thought, as I left the sadist's den. That's the last time, for sure.

The Treatment

Some time went by. I was due to take an extended trip overseas when I realised that some disturbing cavities had appeared in a few of my teeth.

I mulled the thing over and decided that I may as well stick with a sadist I know rather than subject myself to a foreign one. Even then it took two weeks to summon up the courage to make an appointment. But, heroically, I did so. Never let it be said my family lacks courage.

I walked, or rather staggered into the sadist's den one early afternoon. The reason I was a bit unsteady on my feet was that I had consumed a fair amount of rum to give me the afore-mentioned courage.

The assistant sadist looked at me rather oddly, sniffing the air, told me to take a seat and said that I'd be attended to shortly.

I knew this was part of the softening-up process, but I did take a seat and concentrated on what revenge I could conjure up on these purveyors of human misery. Boiling in oil came to mind, but before I could develop upon the theme I was called into the inner sanctum.

I was asked to lie down on the couch. I did so grudgingly. The sadist asked me if I had been drinking. I confirmed that I had. He gave a few deep sighs. I suppose sadists like you to experience every bit of pain that can be involved without your senses being dulled by alcohol.

He asked me to open my mouth. I couldn't. I suddenly had a severe case of lockjaw. In the paternalistic manner these people employ, he said that he could hardly have a look at my teeth if my mouth remained closed. I thought about that and gave in.

He leaned over me.

I screamed.

He said he hadn't done anything yet.

I apologised.

Taking one of those infernal instruments – you know, the ones that are quite sharp with a curved bit on the end – he ventured into the recesses of my mouth.

This time the sadist screamed. Seems I had bitten him on the finger hard enough to draw blood. I apologised again.

By now I'd gathered that the sadist was well and truly miffed.

He had a short consultation with the assistant sadist who gave me one of those pitying looks. I ignored her, went back to thoughts of boiling oil.

The sadist came back with what looked like a huge syringe in his hand. The assistant sadist said not to worry, this would not hurt a bit. She need not have worried.

I'd fainted.

By the time I was back in the land of the living my mouth seemed to be totally separate from the rest of my body. In fact, it did not seem to be part of my body at all. No feeling there whatsoever.

This is where the sadist went into overdrive. The drill was activated. The effect on me was immediate; similar, I assume, to that so well chronicled by Pavlov.

I asked for some time out to attend to a personal hygiene issue. The sadist looked puzzled, but pointed me in the direction of the bathroom-cum-toilet. I repaired there quickly.

The reason for the request was that I seemed to have soiled my underpants. Pavlov never mentions this but perhaps that's because he seems happiest with dogs. A considerable amount of scrubbing and warm water proceeded before I was able (somewhat damply) to resume my position on the couch. This time both the sadist and his assistant sniffed the air in what I can only describe as a highly suspicious and offensive manner.

The assistant sadist advised me to flush my mouth out with the mouthwash. I asked if they had anything stronger. Might as well have been mumbling to the door post. Sadists delight in their work.

The drill started again.

As the sadist bent over towards me, panic set in. My right leg, taking on a life of its own, straightened and caught him in a very sensitive part of his anatomy.

I apologised profusely, but this seemed to have no effect on the sadist or his assistant. Rather, threats were made as regards calling in the police and having me arrested for assault.

My reply was swift. Told them if anyone was being assaulted it was me. With very dangerous implements, no less.

And I was quite prepared to sue.

To make matters worse, the local anaesthetic was wearing off. The sadist limped across and offered to give me another shot. I gave him a look of studied indifference.

He approached again, this time from the side, waving what looked like a syringe one would use to have horses put down.

I fainted again.

By the time I had recovered the job had finally been done. I now had some new fillings in my teeth. Another tooth had been extracted.

To give the sadist his due, he seems to hold no real grudges. Mind you, I'll wait till the fillings stay in place for a while and make sure they don't drop out next time I bite on a piece of bread before I pass the final judgement.

Epilogue

Before I left the sadist's den, he encouraged me to come back in the next few weeks to have my teeth professionally cleaned. Said it would not be all that painful. Said it would help preserve my teeth.

Bugger that.

Dentures have never looked so inviting.

My Town

How does it feel to leave a place where one has lived the best part of one's life? Extremely hard, I'd say, and I know, because I'm just about to do it.

There is a country and western song by Iris DeMent titled exactly the same as this story and probably expresses the feeling better than I ever could. In the final haunting lyrics of the song, Ms DeMent affirms her love for her town and states that it will stay for ever in her heart. My sentiments exactly.

I came to Sydney, Australia, thirty-one years ago. Fell in love with the place at first sight, but there again, who wouldn't? Must be one of the most beautiful and spectacular places in the world.

The town's been good to me, despite some failures on the marital side – but that's my problem, not the fault of my town. She's always been there for me, yet too often I took her for granted.

Till now. Now that I have to leave.

The Sydney I first saw thirty-one years ago has moved on apace. I suppose so have I. In a lot of ways we complemented each other. I built two houses here and helped create two new suburbs. She gave me the incentive to do so. She was the one who offered me the opportunity of a career that I could only dream about before. And I certainly took her up on her offer.

My town has grown. There are now areas which I find hard to relate to because I have not had the opportunity or the motivation to visit them and do so, but my particular part of it will always stay in my heart.

My town is where my son was born. Right there on the

North Shore. I was there for the duration. I was the first person after the midwife to take him and hold him in my arms and feel that indescribable love only a parent can feel for that little being one has helped to bring into the world. The midwife suggested I stick the tip of my little finger in his mouth to give him something to suck on. And he did. Took me five years to break his habit of sucking his thumb after that episode.

It was here that I saw him take his first steps. Here where I heard him utter his first word. 'Dad,' as it happens.

Here is where I saw him through pre- and primary school. Introduced him to football. Coached him and his friends at football for the next few years. And took great pride in his achievements.

Here, also, is where I saw him go to high school, develop as a very promising rugby player, fall in love for the first and only time so far, and become as much a friend as a son.

Yes, I love my town.

I love the colours, the climate, the people – the sight of the Blue Mountains on a clear morning never fails to bring a lump to my throat. The clear blue skies that seem much higher and bigger than anywhere else in the world I have visited.

The jacaranda trees that bring forth their beautiful lilac blooms regularly each November. The wattle trees with their distinct yellow-and-gold blooms – uniquely Australian. The agapanthus that seem to grow in every garden, both lilac and white. And everywhere, those majestic eucalyptuses.

The people of my town are something else in themselves. As varied a bunch as you could ever put together. All nationalities, all creeds, all colours. Multiculturalism in its best form. Sure, you get the odd bad one or two, from all the races in my town, happens anywhere in the world, yet the whole thing works on the basic Aussie principles of 'give everyone a fair go' and 'always help out a mate in trouble'. And it does work well, believe me.

I love the kids who seem to spend most of their time out of

doors rather than staring at a TV screen. The sporting ethos which has made Australia such a respected opponent in so many sports. And even the much-discussed rivalry between my town and Melbourne. I know which one is best – but there again, I'm biased.

The dry, laconic humour of a Sydneysider is something I treasure – especially when arriving back at the airport after a stint abroad, even when going through Customs. Officials completely indifferent to strict formality and willing to share a joke and a laugh with anyone of the same persuasion. Aussies at their best.

I love the sight of the Pacific Ocean from any of my town's beaches. Could stare at it for hours – often have done. Brings a certain peace to the soul.

Even better were the deep-sea fishing excursions where I could spend the best part of the day out on the ocean – but not that far from my town.

In my town I know the best places to visit, whether it be for a recreational break or to get business done. The author Stephen King summed it up best in his novella, *Rita Hayworth and Shawshank Redemption*. Focuses largely on a character serving life in a US penitentiary, but who can get anything for anyone from the outside – for a price, of course. I can identify with that. After that many years one builds a network of contacts and also builds on experience. You know who to see to get the best deal on anything you need, services you need performed, favours that can be cashed in. Moving to a new place means re-engineering all those links in a different environment. Not something achievable in a day or two.

And, of course, there are the friends. Friends that in some cases one did not realise were there but when things got rough gave their help and support. I bless and love them all. And will miss them. Miss them and the kindness and warmth they afforded me. I hope that in the days to come I will still get to see them on the odd occasion.

Why then, I hear you say, am I leaving my town?

Because a greater love has called me away, is the answer. Someone who means absolutely everything to me, for whose sake I'd go anywhere, do anything for, just to be with her. The one I've loved since childhood, with whom I should have spent my life but to my eternal regret did not. The one with whom I intend to spend the rest of my life. The one who makes the rest of the world fade into insignificance.

Even my town.

My Father's Watch

He was a tough one, my father. As strict a disciplinarian as you could ever hope to meet. No wonder we never saw eye to eye.

He was the son of a miner who later became a peasant farmer in pre-war Poland. He probably inherited the traits in his character that particularly irked me from his father – stubbornness; a refusal to give up on anything; a single-minded belief that what he was doing was the right thing, regardless of anybody; and miserliness.

Of course, I didn't realise I'd inherited most of those traits myself.

All I saw in my teenage years was someone with whom I found it increasingly impossible to communicate. Someone who seemed to rub me up the wrong way on just about every topic under the sun on purpose.

I still remember the walloping he gave me the time he caught me smoking at the age of thirteen. He'd given up the habit a few months earlier and, looking back, he obviously resented his son taking it up at the same time.

I remember him making me study when all I wanted to do was play football with the other kids in the street.

I remember him sending me to Polish school on a Saturday morning and forcing me to attend Polish community activities at a time when what I wanted most was to be like any other normal English kid.

I remember the fact that he was so mean with money. I took the first part-time job I could at the age of fifteen just to get financial independence.

I remember him giving me his considered opinion of the girls who began to appear in my life. Opinions which I thought were not just old-fashioned, but completely out of order.

I remember the fact that, although a keen sportsman himself in his youth, he never attended any of the games I played.

I remember the fact that he was never in evidence at any social functions where I would have liked him to be present.

I remember his insistence that I always appear 'smart' in public, no matter what fashion would be dictating to the contrary.

I remember the fact that he would never listen to my arguments and never see my point of view.

Most of all I remember that it was his intransigence on a lot of things that made me leave home for a lengthy spell before my mother's intervention and pleas to return home again.

There are probably more. The list could go on and on.

But, of course, there are things that a teenager overlooks or conveniently forgets, like the fact that this was a guy who fought for his country in World War II and was wounded in battle.

This was a man who was forced thereafter to work on an Austrian farm, and stay there for most of the remainder of the war.

He risked alienation from his father to marry the woman he loved, and loved her throughout their life together and tended her through her final illness and death.

This was a man who, when I got into a slight brush with the law, merely said, 'Guess you're paid up for the guilt that's been eating you up inside for the last month. But why didn't you tell me earlier? Could have saved yourself a lot of worry and heartache.'

This was a man who reinforced in me the pride in the country of his birth and in its culture, which I value so deeply today.

A man who helped my son take his first steps on a visit to Australia some years ago, and later who took my son aside on his last visit to the UK and slipped him £1,000 with an apology that he hadn't remembered to give him regular presents before.

He worked as hard as anyone could to give his family the best start in life possible. Work that involved hard labour, eight-hour rotating shifts, more often than not with overtime thrown in as well, and cycling miles to work and back in all weathers.

He was, when I went through a marital crisis, the first to lend support and assure me that he would be there to support me whatever happened.

In light of all this, all I can say is that I was deeply wrong.

He was right on most matters and certainly on the things that matter.

He taught me so many things: self-discipline, but linked to love and compassion; pride in my ancestry; honour; tolerance. He taught me not to rely on the lottery, but to just get out there and earn your money yourself. He taught me that personal wealth is a thing to be earned, not squandered or used for self-glorification or impressing others. He taught me that the family ethos is one of the most important things in life; that, in the final analysis, you have to stay true to your values.

The list could go on infinitely.

I look back now on all those years and I feel like kicking myself for not seeing the things that should have been so obvious but weren't.

Looking back, I can see that with the effort he was putting in at work, and the effect it was having on him, he'd hardly have had the time or energy to see me play in some immaterial game or some athletics carnival.

I should have realised that a long time ago, but did not. To tell you the truth, I spent too much time thinking about myself, not enough about him.

He and I will never see eye to eye about everything. What father and son ever do?

But I love him.

When he finally retired from work – albeit reluctantly – his employers presented him with a gold watch.

It's engraved with the words 'For Good Service'.

Personally, I reckon that's an understatement on all accounts.

That's why I now wear that watch and wear it with pride, in honour of the guy who brought me into this world, who taught me so much, with whom I've had so many run-ins and misunderstandings, but who I reckon is one of the best ever born.

My father.

The Last Battle

Introduction

Most people believe that the Second World War ended with the unconditional surrender of the Japanese onboard the USS *Missouri* in 1945.

Most people are wrong.

The last battle of World War II was fought not very long ago in Castle Hill, Sydney, New South Wales, Australia.

In the kitchen of my house.

Background

I live alone with just a dog for company. I was married until fairly recently and lived with a wife and son. However, it gradually became apparent that things were not working out as they should. To put it bluntly, my wife and I had grown apart.

It manifested itself mainly in little things. She loved the opera, a branch of the arts that did absolutely nothing for me. On the other hand she had no time for Johnny Cash. Clearly, it was never going to work.

Little things, perhaps, but when added up they can make a difference to two people trying to share a life together. So the upshot was that we decided to separate. Though anti-Johnny Cash sentiment did leave some residual rancour, the separation was fairly amicable, so far as these things ever can be, and I moved out. I bought a house fairly nearby, smaller than the one I was used to, but with a household consisting of just myself it was more than comfortable.

As things turned out the separation was a good move for me. I had my independence back again and my son visited regularly. More importantly, after years of compromise I was now able to do what I liked, how I liked and when I liked, even if it meant playing a little Johnny Cash in the middle of the night.

But I believe that everyone should have a companion. As other human beings were out of the question, an animal seemed to be the perfect answer. Hence the dog.

Wee Jess

'Bitch.'

'Pardon?'

'The male of the species is called a dog. The female is a bitch. Now, do you think you can remember that?'

The speaker was a dog breeder. Most people would proba-bly have been content to describe him as a dour Scot. To me, he was a foul-tempered, foul-mouthed, irascible and cantan-kerous old sod with whom I would normally have nothing to do. But he was a breeder of West Highland terriers. At that time they were fairly rare in Australia and, consequently, much desired by aficionados such as myself. More to the point, one of his bitches was about to whelp shortly and I dearly wanted one of the litter. And if that meant ingratiating myself with the old sod, then ingratiate myself I would.

I had wanted a West Highland terrier for some years, ever since I had seen a British program called *Hamish MacBeth* on the television. Set in some impossibly beautiful location in the Scottish Highlands, the storyline centred around a handsome young policeman. But to me the real star was his West

Highland terrier, called Wee Jock. This dog seemed the absolute epitome of what a dog should be – affectionate, loyal and brave. The perfect companion. I was determined to get one.

'Ever had one of this breed before?' barked the breeder.

'No, but I have had dogs before.'

'Bloody amateur.' He sniffed disdainfully. 'And what will you be wanting a West Highland terrier for?'

'Er… companionship, a good watchdog…'

'Then you're wasting your time,' said the salesman of the year. 'Bloody things lie about the place sleeping most of the day and they're the biggest cowards God ever created. You'd be better off with another breed.'

I was not convinced. One only had to look at one of these terriers strutting round the yard and barking at anything that moved to know that the breeder was wrong. This was a brave breed indeed.

I paid the Scottish usurer a small fortune and agreed to return in six weeks' time to pick up the pup. It would be a bitch as all the males were spoken for already.

'And what are you going to call her?'

'Wee Jessie.'

'God help us.'

I returned in six weeks, picked up the pup and brought her home.

She seemed to fit in well. Contrary to the breeder's forecast she did not sleep all day, but preferred to strut along the fence separating my house from next door's. Unfortunately this had the effect of driving Custer, the neighbour's golden retriever, insane with lust. And it also had the effect of turning Custer into a pale shadow of his former healthy self. With the result that he lost weight to such an alarming extent that the vet had to be called in and promptly put the poor animal on a special diet involving a not insignificant quantity of vitamin pills.

Evenings usually found Wee Jess and myself in the lounge sharing the couch, where she had appropriated one of the cushions. I would normally read a book while she preferred the television, soap operas in particular.

My son called round one day to give her the once over.

'Bit small for a dog,' was his judgement.

'Bitch,' I said instinctively. 'And what do you expect from a West Highland terrier? The Hound of the Baskervilles?'

He mulled that one over.

'And what are you calling her?'

'Wee Jess.'

It's a sad commentary on our (expensive) system of progressive education when one has to describe to one's son the difference between an adjective and the imperative form of the verb. I finally got him to understand.

'Still think it's a daft name, though.'

'Indeed? And what would you have called her?'

'Satan.'

Sometimes I worry about that boy.

The Battle

It had been a very pleasant evening and I did not get home till approximately 2 a.m. When I did, I decided to nip into the kitchen and pour myself a nightcap.

It was then that I came face-to-face with the enemy.

An enormous cockroach was standing in the middle of the floor, my floor, staring at me. I stared right back. And did not like what I saw.

A black shiny body. Antennae which moved, but in different directions to each other. And those ghastly hairy legs.

I decided to make a quick end of it. Picking up a cookery book I lunged at the invader. I was way too slow. The cockroach shot off towards the sink where it buried itself in a deep crevice from which there was no hope of extricating the beast.

I paused, breathing heavenly. Then an idea came to me. I

am a devotee of the Chinese master Sun Tzu, whose treatise, *The Art of War*, is universally acclaimed as the best of that particular genre. I remembered that one of the precepts he tried to instil in his disciples was, 'Know your enemy.' I decided to follow his advice.

To turn on the computer was the work of a matter of seconds. To search the Internet did not take much longer. And there was all the information I needed about cockroaches, including photographs.

Apparently there are three main strains of cockroaches. The American, the German and the Oriental. I immediately discounted the Oriental on the grounds of its size and colouring. The other two were harder to pinpoint, being largely similar in appearance. And with the speed at which this blight on society moved, visual identification would be difficult if not impossible. It was clear that logic was the only answer to the problem facing me.

I considered the American cockroach first. To me, the Americans had always seemed a peaceful nation unless someone got up their collective nose, in which case they were quite prepared to kick ass. True, on occasion they have been known to offer unsolicited and not always universally appreciated assistance in governance to the other less fortunate countries but, in my opinion, always with the best will in the world.

And (this is the clincher) they were our gallant allies in the Second World War, or at least the end of it. Still, better late than never.

I turned my attention to the German cockroach. Although Slav blood flows through my veins, I was determined to be as impartial as possible. Unfortunately this particular cockroach seemed to have a predilection for carving out some Lebensraum. And we all know the consequences of that little experiment in the fairly recent past. Not in my kitchen, pal, I thought to myself.

Then there was the matter of invasion. Unlike the peace-loving Americans, the Germans over the years do not seem to have had any problem with this concept. In invading my kitchen, this particular cockroach was merely acting in keeping with the promptings of its historical genes.

It was obvious that the cockroach in my kitchen was German. And I was faced with the continuation of a conflict that everyone thought had ended in 1945.

I now had the information I required.

So what are you going to do with it, then? the unbidden thought came to me and would not be pushed aside.

Never mind, I'll think of something, I reassured myself.

I returned to the kitchen only to find that the damn thing had returned. I realised I would need to summon up the heavy artillery. Picking up Wee Jess from her customary position on the couch, I returned to the kitchen. The enemy had not moved.

'Right, Wee Jess,' I whispered. 'This is your big moment.'

I put her on the floor, gave her a light shove in the direction of the enemy and shouted '*Kill!*' at the top of my voice. Wee Jess gave a yelp and shot off in the direction of the lounge, the cockroach scuttled back in the direction of its hiding place, and I was left in the middle like a shag on a rock, feeling like a right dill.

I stormed into the lounge. Wee Jess had taken refuge underneath the cushion. You could tell where she was by the vibrations.

'Stop trembling and come out, you little coward!'

The only response was an increased level of vibration. Perhaps the breeder had been right after all. What I do know is that you'll never hear me singing 'Scotland the Brave' ever again. At this point I realised that I was on my own. I would have to face the enemy. Alone. I made my way back to the kitchen. There, everything was quiet – no sign of anyone or any thing.

I decided to make myself a cup of coffee to calm the nerves.

I got the coffee and the milk and set about boiling the water. When this was ready, I took a careful look around. All clear.

I hefted the kettle and tipped it over the mug. The cockroach chose that moment to put in an appearance, hustling across the sink directly in front of me. My right arm jerked and deposited half a cup of scalding water on my left hand. I immediately shoved the hand under a running cold tap while trying to monitor the movements of the cockroach. It appeared to have taken shelter underneath the microwave.

I examined the microwave carefully, even raising it slightly to get a better look. Still no cockroach. I picked the appliance up bodily to get a better look. The cockroach leapt out and ran at me. I promptly dropped the microwave. Right on to my left foot, fracturing the big toe.

OK, I thought. No more Mr Nice Guy. The gloves are well and truly off.

I picked up a very sharp boning knife. The cockroach, perhaps exhausted as well, came to a stop in the middle of the floor. I edged my way towards it. When I thought I was in range, I collected myself and made a desperate lunge towards my tormentor.

Unfortunately my fractured toe came into play at this moment. I slipped, fell awkwardly and stabbed myself in the left arm. The cockroach disappeared.

I was ready to give in. If I'd had a white flag I'd have probably flown it there and then. I made a rough bandage for my arm, restored the microwave to its normal position and mopped up the blood as best I could.

They say that when the world ends, it will not be with a bang, but a whimper. That may or may not be true. All I know is that, as I limped away from the scene of carnage that was my kitchen, there was a distinct crunch. I looked under my shoes. There, squashed under the sole of one of them, was my arch enemy.

'Did you give him a decent burial?' some idiot once asked.

'Bugger that for a lark,' I answered.

I called in to the Emergency Department of the local hospital as soon as I could. My left foot was soon encased in a plaster cast while stitches held together the knife wound. They said that while the scald was obviously painful, it was not considered serious enough to warrant further treatment. They gave me some extra strong painkillers instead.

'How did you manage all that anyway?' asked the bemused duty nurse as I was leaving.

'Just a slight altercation,' I replied.

And so ended the last battle.

The Medal

Some days later I was browsing through the stalls of the local markets. This is one of my favourite pastimes, as one can never predict what one may find.

This time I came across one full of military memorabilia. Of special interest to me was a cardboard box containing a fairly large collection of military medals. I looked for the owner. The only candidate seemed to be a rather unkempt young man with a severe skin complaint, who was engrossed in the latest version of a Superman comic while busily exploring his nasal cavities with his right forefinger.

'Excuse me,' I said, 'but are you the manager?'

'Yeah, you could say that,' came the reply.

I mentally added halitosis to my inventory of the young man's health issues.

'Good, good,' I said. 'I'm particularly interested in the medals. Is this the total sum of your offerings?'

'What?' said the entrepreneur.

I sighed. 'Is this the lot or do you have any more?'

'Why didn't you say so? Nah, that's the lot. Want me to help you look through them?'

A picture of his right forefinger appeared in my mind.

'No, no, thank you very much,' I said hastily. 'I'll just have a quiet browse.'

'Suit yourself,' he said, and returned to his comic and nasal cavities.

Finally I found what I was looking for. Not gaudy, but colourful in a dignified way. It looked fairly old.

'Which war is this one from, do you know?' I asked the entrepreneur.

'Haven't got a clue, mate, but judging by the state of it, probably from sometime in the last century. My guess would be Iraq.'

As I limped away I reflected that a rudimentary knowledge of history and/or current affairs were not strictly necessary prerequisites to enter into business.

Reminiscences

With all the recent trauma I decided on a short break up the coast. I picked on Dingo's Knob because:

a)   I'd been there before and liked the place;

b)   the scenery was fantastic;

c)   the locals were friendly;

d)   the place boasted a decent social and recreation club with a bistro attached;

e)   I had a few drinking mates there from earlier visits.

I arrived a couple of days before Anzac Day, the most sacred day in the Antipodean calendar, which honours all who served in previous and current wars. It's a day when old uniforms are pulled out of mothballs and once again proudly worn. Needless to say, it's a day when medals are just as proudly displayed.

And, as I entered the Dingo's Knob Social and Recreation

Club, I was wearing my medal.

The place was packed to the rafters. Two of my drinking mates, Bruce and Kevin, were already at one of the tables, accompanied by two people I had never seen before. One was a tall, beefy man, the other, a petite brunette, appeared to be his wife. I made my way across to join them.

'G'day, Harry,' came the greeting from Kevin and Bruce.

'G'day, lads.' I looked somewhat quizzically at the other members of the group.

Bruce caught my look.

'Harry, I'd like you to meet—'

'Leroy Q Schwarzkopf,' broke in the big man. 'And the pretty filly here is my wife, Mary Lou. Ain't she jest the purtiest thing you've ever seen, Hank?'

The purtiest thing tittered. I winced. Rhyming slang is still quite popular in Australia and there are too many words which rhyme with Hank for me to be entirely happy with this arrangement. As it was, I could see Kevin and Bruce already nudging each other and exchanging sly grins.

'The name is Harry, Leroy. *Harry*,' I said.

'Sure, whatever you say, Hank. Mary Lou and I are over here on vacation. We're from Rounder Bend, West Arkansas, not all that far from the Texas border. I expect you've heard of it?'

I confessed that I had not. He seemed disappointed till I told him I'd make a point of visiting one day.

That cheered him up. 'Why, Mary Lou and I would love you come round and stay a spell. Enjoy some southern hospitality. Have a look round. Best cotton-picking little town in all of West Arkansas, is Rounder Bend.'

We drank a toast to Rounder Bend.

As I mentioned earlier, the place was packed to the rafters. The noise was such that in some cases it was difficult to hear or understand the other person. To add to all this, sometimes all five of us were talking at the same time. It was inevitable, therefore, that there would be some measure of confusion and at times whole phrases or even sentences would be lost in the general din.

Leroy was looking at my medal.

'You've seen some action then, fella?' It was a half-statement, half-question.

'You can say that again, Leroy,' was my rejoinder. 'You can say that again.' I spoke with feeling because I still couldn't forget that blasted cockroach.

'What rank were you, Hank, if you don't mind me asking?' from Leroy.

'Say, Harry, settle an argument for us, will you? Do you own the house here or are you a tenant?' from Bruce.

'And how do you like Australia, Mary...' Kevin had obviously forgotten the second part of her name.

'Lou,' I filled him in.

'Tenant,' I told Bruce.

'We don't normally talk about it, Leroy.' I'd spent my national service time peeling potatoes in a camp just outside Kempsey and the fewer people who knew about that the better, as far as I was concerned.

'But which branch of the forces were you with?' pursued Leroy.

'Just getting some beers in, Harry,' shouted Kevin across the table. 'What would you like, premium or special?'

'Special,' I replied. 'And keep your voice down, will you?'

'Sorry, Leroy,' I said. 'You were asking?'

'No, it's all clear now, Hank.' He patted his nose knowingly. 'Tell me confidentially, Hank, you ever been to the Middle East?'

I was slightly puzzled at this change of topic, but gave it some thought.

'I have, Leroy.' Which was true. We'd had a short refuelling stopover in Abu Dhabi or Muscat or Bahrain or some other sweat hole on the Sydney–Heathrow run. I remember there were problems at the airport that day – the air conditioning had broken down, none of the bars were open and religious law prevented me from drinking even my own duty-free hooch in public. I remember being ecstatic when the plane took off again.

'And what did you think of the place and our Ay-rab friends?'

I leaned forward confidentially.

'To be frank, Leroy, I hated the – hell of a racket here tonight – place. Couldn't wait to get out of it. As regards the people, the one thing I can't forgive or forget is that they wouldn't let me have a drink for hours.'

The big man looked incredulous.

'You mean they stopped you from drinking all that time?' His face turned beetroot red. 'The bastards!' he spat with venom. 'Now I know what we're fighting for and the sort of people we're up against.'

'Hey, Harry, hear you had a spot of trouble with the wild-life.' Loud laughter from Kevin and Bruce.

'That ain't funny, fellas.' Leroy had obviously taken me to heart.

'It's OK, Leroy, just some harmless joshing.'

'You got captured and, er… interrogated? My God, what sort of people were you dealing with?'

'Come on, tell us about your run-in with the beast, Harry' begged Kevin.

'Cocky bastard. He's what put me in hospital.'

I showed them the scar on my left arm.

Leroy was close to apoplexy and his knuckles had turned white. He insisted on buying me a triple whisky while casting a belligerent eye at the somewhat swarthy waiter serving us.

'Let's change the subject,' said Mary Lou, clearly worried by the rising level of Leroy's blood pressure.

'Tell us about your wife, Hank.'

'Nice dog you have there, Harry,' observed Bruce.

'Bitch,' I said mechanically. 'Might be good-looking, but she let me down badly just when I needed her most.'

'That's so sad, isn't it, Leroy?' from the tender-hearted Mary Lou.

'Seems you and your wife don't get on too well,' said Leroy.

'We've split up, in fact. Separated.'

'That's a helluva big step, Hank,' advised Leroy. 'D'yall think you can get back together again?'

'Doubt it very much, Leroy. I'll tell you something I haven't told anyone else before.' Now this was the booze talking. I leaned forward and carefully checked to see that no one could overhear. 'This is almost impossible to believe, but I know it for a fact because she even told me: that woman does not like Johnny Cash!'

For a few moments I was sure we'd have to call an ambulance. And I was blaming myself. Seems you just do not tell a West Arkansas boy one of his state's greatest heroes has been insulted by some foreign woman. It's akin to throwing Mom's apple pie uneaten into the garbage.

It took all four of us quite a while to calm Leroy down. Actually it was three because Mary Lou kept bursting into floods of tears and moaning, 'How could she? How could she?'

Bruce tried to change the topic.

'Getting any money out of the government, Harry?'

'Only the usual pittance, Bruce.' I was on unemployment relief.

'How about disability?' asked Leroy.

'You'd have to be joking,' I replied.

'But surely, after all you've been through, they owe you something extra?' Again, half-statement, half-question.

'Well, I sure as hell won't hold my breath waiting for it,' I replied.

'Well, I'll make sure this won't go unrewarded, Hank, you can bet your life on that. Good God, man, you're a goddam hero.'

I figured that this was definitely the booze talking. We parted shortly afterwards with the usual mutual exhortations to keep in touch and to visit some time. Small chance of that happening, I thought.

As we staggered out through the car park, Leroy pulled me to one side.

'Didn't want to ask in front of Mary Lou, but can you tell me one thing?'

'Sure, ol' buddy, ol' pal.'

'When your wife told you… told you… you know, those… things…' his voice failed him.

'You mean about Johnny Cash?'

For a moment I thought he was going to have another attack, but he pulled himself together.

'Did you consider giving her a good horse-whipping?'

'No, Leroy, that's not me.'

'No, I didn't think so,' said Leroy as we shook hands in goodbye.

We went our separate ways. The last thing I heard was Leroy's voice.

'Pity.'

The Americans

Some four months had passed since that evening in Dingo's Knob and Leroy was just a dim, if pleasant, memory. To be honest, I never expected to hear from him again. It was with some surprise, therefore, that one day in August I received a letter postmarked Little Rock, Arkansas, USA. On opening it I found:

a) a cheque for US$15,000 made out to me and drawn on the account of the Rounder Bend Veterans' Association at some bank in Little Rock, Arkansas;

b) a newspaper cutting from *The Rounder Bend Bugle and Clarion* (best little newspaper in all of West Arkansas);

c) a letter from Leroy Q Schwarzkopf.

I read the cutting first.

LOCALS MEET AUSTRALIAN WAR HERO

My wife, Mary Lou, and I have recently returned from a wonderful vacation in Dingo's Knob, Queensland, Australia. The weather and the scenery are even better than we were led to believe and the locals every bit as friendly and as hospitable as folks back home.

But what really made this vacation so special for us was meeting a genuine war hero.

A lieutenant in the Australian Special Forces (similar to our Green Berets), this man has seen and experienced at first hand the full horrors of war in the Middle East. Or, as he himself so eloquently put it, 'the hell of Iraq.'

Though tortured and wounded by an arrogant and sadistic interrogator, he came through the ordeal in typically heroic fashion.

This quiet, unassuming and modest man, while carrying with him the burden of painful memories, nevertheless seems to harbour no bitterness, even towards his own government which has treated him so shamefully, allowing him just a pittance to live on.

His wife has left him following an altercation involving his love and admiration for this state's greatest hero, Johnny Cash, and now he lives alone with just his small dog for company.

This man is a hero, ladies and gentlemen, and deserves better from all of us.

Lieutenant, we salute you!

I was quite taken with this article until I realised they were talking about me. I re-read it. Certainly the words, phrases and even sentences were as I remembered them, but everything seemed to be out of context, with the result that what I was reading in no way reflected what was meant or intended at the time. At best, it had all been completely misconstrued. I resolved to put this right at the earliest opportunity.

I picked up Leroy's letter.

Dear Hank (or should that be Good day, y'all),

No doubt you're surprised to hear from me after all this time, but you'll be even more surprised when you get the rest of the news. You'll have read by now the letter I sent to the *Bugle and Clarion*. It must have struck a chord somewhere because it was picked up by the Little Rock press and then syndicated clear across all the southern States (and Kansas, for some reason or other).

Before we knew it, we had more cash donations than a dog has fleas in the summertime. But that's not all. You seem to have become a cult figure with the ladies – some of them want to mother you, some to marry you, some both. I'll send you some of the letters some time – hot stuff, let me tell you. Anyway, they all seem to think that living alone you must at least be starving and certainly not able to look after yourself. The parcels began to arrive just over two months ago and we've been deluged since to the point where we did not know what to do with all the stuff.

It was Mary Lou's idea to open the 'Lieutenant Harry Memorial Shop' right here in Rounder Bend, selling all the stuff we were getting at low prices to the less advantaged members of our community. This has proved exceedingly popular and made you even more of a hero to people than before, if that were possible. I swear, and I'm not joshing you here, the day you set foot in Rounder Bend the good folks will probably elect you mayor unanimously.

Anyway, with the popularity of the Lieutenant Harry Memorial Shop being what it is, the first franchise should start operations in Baton Rouge, Louisiana before Christmas, with Jackson, Mississippi opening in February and Memphis, Tennessee and Wichita, Kansas coming on stream by Easter.

Needless to say, Mary Lou has long since given up her former job as a dental receptionist and now works on these projects full-time. Goddammit, that woman's making more money than me!

But on to more important things. You're in great demand on the after-dinner speaking circuit. This is where the real money is, old buddy. I've had so many Veterans' Associations squabbling over you like bobcats in a gunny sack it's about time we addressed this problem. As soon as you can make it, I'll arrange an all-expenses-paid ticket from Sydney to Little Rock via Houston and Dallas and we can cut a schedule for the first round of speeches. Just make sure you make it soon. That'll be it for now, old pal. Hope to see you in the very near future. I think Mary Lou wants to scribble a few words as well, so I'll sign off here.

Leroy Q Schwarzkopf

Postscript

Hank, I'm looking forward so much to seeing you again. Leroy and I think you're the best thing ever to happen to us. There are quite a few young ladies who have expressed a very strong desire to meet you, so you'll be a busy man when you get here. By the way, I bet you'll never guess what the most popular line in the shop at the moment is – it's a CD of Johnny Cash's *Greatest Hits*. I think Leroy wants to add another few words, so I'll say bye for now. Love, Mary Lou.

Forgot to mention this, Hank, but when the news first broke some of the good ol' boys took things to heart and wanted to go visit your ex-wife. I managed to put a stop to that nonsense but you might just mention to her that leaving the southern States, and particularly Arkansas, off her list of places to visit might be a shrewd move in the circumstances. Leroy.

I read the letter again, quite a few times. Then I read the newspaper cutting again a few times.

By then I was convinced that perhaps I had been a bit hasty

in my original judgement. Certainly the words were as I remembered them. Perhaps Leroy's recollection was more reliable than mine. Perhaps…

What the hell.

I picked up a pen and started on my letter of acceptance.

Epilogue

Well, that's it.

I sold Wee Jess, at an inflated price, to another Scotsman (poetic justice) looking for an affectionate and loyal animal who would make a good guard dog. I figured that by the time he discovered that she was an out-and-out coward I'd be long gone. Custer was completely devastated at the loss of his only love and the vet had to be summoned yet again.

I let the house on a long lease. Before handing over the keys to the tenants I made sure the place was completely fumigated. We don't want a repeat of the last battle, do we?

The taxi taking me to the airport should be here any moment. I have only one worry in the whole world: what on earth am I going to talk about at these after-dinner speeches?

Lightning Source UK Ltd.
Milton Keynes UK
28 November 2009

146820UK00001B/14/A